*We have the best time reading the Magic Tree House series. Jack and Annie have become household names.*—K. Moore

*You should have been in the classroom when I discovered and shared with them that there were indeed four more [books]. They literally stood and cheered.*—C. Garrison

*[My students] choose your books to reread during free time, which is the greatest compliment of all.*—N. Ruud

*Your books have become so popular in our school that the shelf life of one of your books is about five seconds.*—C. Dailey

Dear Readers,

Imagine a time in Europe over a thousand years ago, when every single book had to be written by hand on animal skins, and writers had to make their ink and paints from plants and minerals. In spite of these hardships, Christian monks in Europe—especially in Ireland— made decorated, or "illuminated" manuscripts, which are some of the most beautiful books the world has ever seen.

Now imagine a warship that can travel far across rough seas, weather terrible storms, and land on rocky coasts. The Vikings of Scandinavia made such ships <u>completely by hand</u>. They were the most elegant sailing vessels of all time.

In the last few years, I've seen illuminated manuscripts at the British Museum in London, and Viking warships at the Viking Ship Museum in Oslo, Norway. Ever since, I have wanted to write about both of these wonders. Finally, this book has given me that opportunity.

I hope you find them as "wonder-full" as I do.

All my best,

Mary Pope Osborne

# Viking Ships at Sunrise

by Mary Pope Osborne
illustrated by Sal Murdocca

A STEPPING STONE BOOK™
Random House  New York

*To Benjamin Dicker*

Text copyright © 1998 by Mary Pope Osborne.
Illustrations copyright © 1998 by Sal Murdocca.

All rights reserved under International and Pan-American Copyright Conventions.
Published in the United States by Random House, Inc., New York, and simultaneously in Canada by Random House of Canada Limited, Toronto.

www.randomhouse.com/magictreehouse/

*Library of Congress Cataloging-in-Publication Data*
Osborne, Mary Pope.
Viking ships at sunrise / by Mary Pope Osborne ; illustrated by Sal Murdocca.
p.  cm. — (Magic tree house ; #15)  "A Stepping Stone book."  Summary: Their magic tree house takes Jack and Annie back to a monastery in medieval Ireland, where they try to retrieve a lost book while being menaced by Viking raiders.
ISBN 0-679-89061-0 (pbk.) — ISBN 0-679-99061-5 (lib. bdg.)
[1. Vikings—Fiction.  2. Monasteries—Fiction.  3. Ireland—Fiction.
4. Time travel—Fiction.  5. Magic—Fiction.  6. Tree houses—Fiction.]
I. Murdocca, Sal, ill. II. Title. III. Series: Osborne, Mary Pope. Magic tree house series ; 15.  PZ7.081167Vh  1998  [Fic]—dc21  98-23602

Printed in the United States of America    13  15  17  19  20  18  16  14  12

Random House, Inc.  New York, Toronto, London, Sydney, Auckland

A STEPPING STONE BOOK is a trademark of Random House, Inc.

# Contents

# VIKING SHIPS
## AT SUNRISE

# Prologue

One summer day in Frog Creek, Pennsylvania, a mysterious tree house appeared in the woods.

Eight-year-old Jack and his seven-year-old sister, Annie, climbed into the tree house. They found that it was filled with books.

Jack and Annie soon discovered that the tree house was magic. It could take them to the places in the books. All they had to do was to point to a picture and wish to go there.

1

Along the way, they discovered that the tree house belongs to Morgan le Fay. Morgan is a magical librarian from the time of King Arthur. She travels through time and space, gathering books.

In the Magic Tree House Books #8–12, Jack and Annie solved four ancient riddles and became Master Librarians. To help them in their *future* tasks, Morgan gave Jack and Annie secret library cards with the letters M L on them.

As Master Librarians, Jack and Annie must go on four missions to save stories from ancient libraries. They have already brought back a scroll from an ancient Roman town and a bamboo book from ancient China. Now, they are about to head out on their third mission…

# 1

## Before Dawn

Jack opened his eyes.

A thin gray light came through his window. His clock read 5 A.M. All was quiet.

*Today we're going to ancient Ireland*, he thought, *back more than a thousand years*.

Morgan le Fay had told him that it was a very dangerous time, with Vikings raiding the coasts.

"You awake?" came a whisper.

Annie stood in his doorway. She was

dressed and ready to go.

"Yeah, meet you outside," said Jack as he climbed out of bed.

He pulled on his jeans, T-shirt, and sneakers. He put his secret library card into his backpack with his notebook and pencil. Then he hurried downstairs.

Annie was waiting for him in their yard.

The air was damp and misty.

"Ready?" she asked.

Jack took a deep breath.

"I guess," he said. He was a little worried about the Vikings.

They walked silently over the dewy grass. Then they ran up their street and into the Frog Creek woods.

Mist clung to the trees as they walked through the dark woods.

"It's hard to see," said Jack.

"Where's the tree house?" asked Annie.

"I have no idea," said Jack.

Just then something fell in front of them.

*"Watch out!"* shouted Jack. He covered his head.

"The ladder!" cried Annie.

Jack opened his eyes.

The rope ladder from the magic tree house dangled in front of them.

Jack looked up. The tree house was hidden in the mist.

"Come on, let's go," said Annie.

She grabbed the ladder and started up. Jack followed.

They climbed through the wet air and into the tree house.

"Hello," said Morgan. "I'm glad to see you."

She was sitting in the corner. At her feet were the scroll they'd brought back from Roman times and the bamboo book from ancient China.

"I'm so glad to see *you*," said Jack.

"Me too," said Annie.

"It's good that you both came early," said Morgan.

She reached into the folds of her robe and pulled out a piece of paper.

"Here's the ancient story you must find today," she said.

Morgan handed the paper to Jack. On it were the words:

erpens Magna

The mysterious writing reminded Jack of

the writing from their trip to the Roman town of Pompeii.

"That looks like Latin," he said.

"Very good," said Morgan. "It *is* Latin."

"But I thought they spoke Latin in ancient Rome," said Annie. "Aren't we going to Ireland?"

"You are," said Morgan. "But during the Dark Ages in Europe, educated people wrote in Latin."

"The *Dark* Ages?" said Jack.

"Yes," said Morgan. "The time after the fall of the Roman Empire."

"Why is it called *dark?*" said Jack.

"It was a difficult time," said Morgan. "People had to work very hard just to feed and clothe themselves. There was not a lot of time for playing, learning, or making art and music."

Morgan pulled a book from her robe.

"Your research," she said, handing it to Annie. The title read: *Ireland Long Ago.*

"Remember," said Morgan. "Your research book will guide you. But in your darkest hour—"

"Only the ancient story can save us," Jack and Annie said together.

"And remember this," said Morgan. "It must be your *darkest* hour, when there is no hope left. If you ask for help too soon, it will not come."

"And we have to find the story *first*," said Annie.

"That is true," said Morgan. "Do you have your secret library cards?"

Jack and Annie nodded.

"Show them to the wisest person you meet," said Morgan.

"Don't worry," said Annie. "I think we're ready now."

Annie pointed at the cover of the Ireland book.

"I wish we could go there," she said. She gave Morgan a little wave. "See you soon."

"Good luck!" said Morgan.

The wind started to blow.

The tree house started to spin.

It spun faster and faster.

Then everything was still.

Absolutely still.

# 2

## The Steep Climb

Jack opened his eyes.

The light was still gray, but the air was even damper and colder than in Frog Creek.

"Wow, I'm in a long dress," said Annie. "It's scratchy. Hey, I've got a little purse on my belt. It has my library card in it!"

Jack looked down at his own clothes.

He was wearing a shirt and trousers, made of heavy wool. He also wore leather slippers. And in place of his backpack was a leather bag.

"Wow," said Annie, looking out the window. "This really looks like the Dark Ages."

Jack looked out, too. He couldn't see anything through the mist.

"It's just because the sun's not up yet," he said. "I'd better check the book."

Annie handed the Ireland book to Jack. He opened it and read aloud:

> The early Middle Ages were once known as the "Dark Ages" because learning and culture nearly vanished throughout Europe. Scholars today praise the brave Irish monks who helped keep Western civilization alive.

"What do 'civilization' and 'monks' mean?" asked Annie.

12

"I think civilization is when people have books and art and good manners," said Jack. "Monks are religious people who spend their time praying and reading and helping people."

"Well, I don't see any civilization *or* monks out there," said Annie, pointing at the mist.

Jack pulled out his notebook. He wrote:

brave monks in Ireland

Then he looked at Annie. "If we find civilization, I think we'll find the lost story," he said.

"Let's go," said Annie. She lifted her skirt and climbed out the window.

Jack read more in the Ireland book.

> **The monks copied the ancient writings of the Western world. Before printing was invented, all books had to be written and copied by hand.**

"Hey, we're on a cliff!" Annie called from outside. "Above the ocean!"

"Be careful!" said Jack.

He stuffed the Ireland book and his notebook into his leather bag. Then he climbed out the window.

Annie was peering over the edge. Jack looked, too.

There was a rocky shore twenty feet below. Waves slapped against the rocks. Sea gulls swooped and glided above the sea.

"It doesn't look like there's any civilization down *there*," said Jack.

"Maybe we should climb those," said Annie. She pointed to steep steps cut into the cliff.

Jack looked up. The cliff also rose above them in the mist.

"We better wait till the sun comes up," he said.

"Let's just go super slow," said Annie. She started up the stone steps.

"Wait, Annie!" said Jack. "They might be slippery."

"Whoa!" she said, almost falling backward. "I tripped on my darn dress!"

"I told you to *wait*," Jack said. "It's too dangerous."

Just then something fell from above.

"Watch it!" said Jack. He put his hands over his head.

"Hey, it's a rope!" said Annie.

Jack saw a thick rope dangling down the stairs.

"Where'd this come from?" he asked.

"It's like when Morgan dropped the ladder to us," said Annie. "I bet someone's trying to help us."

"Yeah, but who?" said Jack.

"Let's find out," said Annie. She grabbed the rope. "I'll use it first. Once I'm at the top, you can come after me."

"Okay, but hurry," he said. "And be very careful." Jack waited as Annie started climbing up the steps.

Annie held on to the rope as she climbed slowly up the stairs. Soon she vanished over the top of the cliff.

"What's up there?" Jack shouted. But his voice was lost in the sound of the waves.

He grabbed the rope and started up the steep steps. At the top of the cliff, he pulled himself over the edge.

"Aha!" boomed a deep, jolly voice. "It's another little invader!"

# 3

## Brother Patrick

Jack's glasses were wet with mist. He quickly wiped them, then looked up.

A man in a brown robe stood before him. The man had a round red face. He was bald, except for a fringe of hair around his head.

Nearby the rope was tied around a tree.

"I—I'm not an invader," said Jack.

"He's *Jack!*" said Annie. She was standing behind the man. "I'm Annie. We're from Frog Creek, Pennsylvania."

"We—we come in peace," stammered Jack.

The man's blue eyes twinkled.

"Oh, do you now?" he said. "I wondered what was going on. I had dropped the rope so I could climb down the steps. But *you* two grabbed it instead. How in the world did you get on this island?"

Jack stared at the man. He didn't know how to explain the magic tree house.

"In our boat," Annie said quickly.

The man looked puzzled. "Not many boats can come ashore at this dark, early hour."

"Well, we're very good sailors," said Annie.

*Oh, brother*, thought Jack. He hoped their sailing skills wouldn't be tested.

"Where exactly are we?" asked Annie.

"And who exactly are you?"

"You're on an island off the coast of Ireland," the man said. "And I am Brother Patrick."

"Whose brother are you?" said Annie.

The monk smiled. "The 'brother' means I'm a Christian monk."

"Oh, you're one of the monks who saved civilization!" said Annie.

The man smiled again.

Annie turned to Jack and whispered, "Let's show him our cards. I trust him."

"Okay," said Jack. He trusted the monk, too.

They both pulled out their secret library cards and showed them to Brother Patrick.

The **M**'s and **L**'s for *Master Librarian* shined in the gray light.

The monk looked at them and bowed his head.

"Welcome, my friends," he said.

"Thank you," said Jack and Annie.

"I did not truly think you were invaders," said Brother Patrick. "But on our small island, we are careful of strangers."

"Why?" said Annie.

"There are terrible stories about Viking raiders," he said. "When we see their serpent ships, we must hide or be taken as slaves."

"Serpent ships?" said Jack.

"The prows of their ships are often carved in the shape of a serpent's head," said Brother Patrick. "I am afraid it stands for their fierce, cold-blooded ways."

Jack looked at the misty gray sea.

"Do not worry," said Brother Patrick. "They cannot land safely on this island before daylight. They're not as good sailors as some people." He winked at Annie.

"Too bad for them," she said cheerfully.

"But tell me, why have you come here?" asked Brother Patrick.

"Oh," said Jack. "I almost forgot."

He pulled Morgan's paper from his leather bag. He showed the Latin words to the monk.

erpens **Magna**

"This is the title of a story that we have to take back to our friend and teacher, Morgan le Fay," said Annie.

"I see..." said Brother Patrick. He gave Jack and Annie a mysterious look.

*What's he thinking?* Jack wondered.

But the monk changed the subject.

"I think you would like to visit our monastery," he said.

"What's that?" said Annie.

"The place where we monks live and work," said Brother Patrick. "Come."

"But the sun's not up yet," said Jack. "Won't the others be asleep?"

"Oh, no," said Brother Patrick. "In the summer, we rise long before daylight. We have much to do. You'll see."

The monk led them up a dirt path. Jack hoped their book was at the monastery. He wanted to leave the gloomy island with its threat of Viking invaders as soon as possible.

A low bell started to ring. Jack saw a lonely church steeple against the gray sky ahead.

# 4

## Books of Wonder

The monastery had a stone wall all around it.

Brother Patrick took Jack and Annie through the gate. Beyond the gate was a small church with a hanging bell.

There was also a vegetable garden and six stone huts shaped like giant beehives.

"We grow all our own food," said Brother Patrick. "Carrots, turnips, spinach, wheat, and beans."

He led them to the entrance of the first

hut. Jack and Annie peeked inside. A monk was pulling flat bread from a low stone oven.

"This is our bakery," Brother Patrick said.

"It smells good!" said Annie.

"Come along," Brother Patrick said.

He pointed to each hut as they passed.

"There are our sleeping quarters," he said. "And that's where we spin our cloth. In here, we cobble our sandals. There we carve our wooden tools."

In each of the huts, Jack and Annie could see monks. They were busy spinning or cobbling or carving.

Finally, Brother Patrick came to the largest beehive-like hut.

"I have saved the best for last," he said.

"This is where we do our most important work."

He stepped inside.

Jack and Annie followed.

The hut was warm and peaceful, yet very alive. It glowed with the golden light of many candles.

Monks sat at wooden tables. Some were reading. Others played chess. Best of all, some were writing and painting in books.

"This is our library," said Brother Patrick. "Here we study math, history, and poetry. We play chess. And we make books."

"Jack," said Annie. "I think this is it."

"What?" said Jack.

*"Civilization!"* said Annie.

Brother Patrick laughed.

"Yes, this is where civilization hides," he

said. "On top of our lonely island in the sea."

"Oh, man," said Jack. "I love this place."

"What kind of books do you make here?" asked Annie.

"Books of wonder," said Brother Patrick. "We record Christian stories as well as the old myths of Ireland."

"Myths?" said Jack.

"Yes," said Brother Patrick. "They were gathered from our storytellers—the old women who sing the tales of long ago, when people believed in magic."

"Wow," said Annie.

"Come," said Brother Patrick, "look at the book of Brother Michael. He has worked on it his whole life."

Brother Patrick led Jack and Annie over to an old monk. The monk was painting a blue border around one of the pages in a book.

"Michael, these two Master Librarians from faraway would like to see your work," said Brother Patrick.

The old monk looked up at Jack and Annie. His wrinkled face broke into a smile.

"Welcome," said Brother Michael in a thin, shaky voice.

"Hi," said Annie.

Brother Michael showed them the cover of his book. It was decorated with gleaming red and blue jewels.

Then he turned the pages. Each was covered with fancy writing and delicate paintings in green, gold, and blue.

"I wish I could paint like that," said Annie.

"It's beautiful," whispered Jack.

"Thank you," said Brother Michael.

"How do you make a book like this?" asked Annie.

"I write on sheepskin and use goose quill pens," said Brother Michael. "My paints are made of earth and plants."

"Wow," said Annie.

"Show Michael what you are seeking," Brother Patrick said.

"Oh, right!" said Jack. He pulled out the paper Morgan had given them. He showed the Latin writing to the old monk.

Brother Michael nodded.

"Yes," he said with a smile. "I know that one quite well."

Brother Michael turned to the page he had

been painting with a blue border. He pointed to the writing at the top of the page.

"Oh, man," whispered Jack.

The words were:

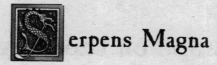erpens Magna

# 5

## Warships on the Waves

"We found our story!" said Jack.

"Yay!" said Annie.

"Indeed," said Brother Patrick. "But alas, Brother Michael has not yet completed his work. You will have to return for it."

"Oh, shoot," said Annie.

Jack was disappointed, too.

"I don't know if we'll be able to come back," he said.

"I don't know if we can even leave without the story," said Annie.

Brother Patrick looked puzzled.

The two kids looked at each other, then back at Brother Patrick. It was too hard to explain about the tree house and how the magic worked.

Jack shrugged.

"We'll just have to try," he said.

Outside, the church bell began ringing.

"It is time now for our sunrise prayers," said Brother Patrick. "Will you join us?"

"Thanks, but we better try to go home now," said Jack.

Brother Patrick nodded and led them into the garden. When he opened the gate, they stopped.

The horizon glowed pink and purple. The

sun had started to rise.

No one spoke as the great, fiery ball rose slowly over the ocean.

Finally, Brother Patrick broke the silence. "Shine, O light of the sun," he said softly, "on this day filled with wonder."

"That's beautiful," said Annie.

Jack smiled. He agreed.

Brother Patrick turned to them. "It is such sights as this that inspire our book-making," he said. "Now go, and may God be with you on your voyage home."

"Thanks," said Jack and Annie.

"Do you need me to guide you to your boat?" he asked.

"I don't think so," said Jack.

"Follow the path to the top of the cliff," said Brother Patrick. "Then use my rope to help you down the steps."

"Okay," said Annie. "Bye!" And she went through the gate.

Jack wanted to go home, but he hated leaving the monastery. It was filled with people doing his favorite things: reading and learning.

"I really like it here," he said to Brother Patrick.

"I'm glad. But you must go now, while the weather is with you," said the monk. *"Everything can change in an instant."*

Then Brother Patrick turned and went into the church.

Jack hurried out the gate. Before he went further, he stopped and pulled out his notebook.

He quickly made two lists:

**To make a book**
sheepskin
goose quill
paints

**To make paint**
earth
plants

"Come on!" Annie called from the top of the steps.

"Coming," Jack called.

He put away his notebook and ran along the dirt path to the edge of the cliff.

Overhead, flocks of gulls circled in the purple sky. Their cries sounded like screams.

"What's wrong with them?" Jack said.

"Maybe they always do this at sunrise," said Annie. "Let me go first."

Clutching the rope, she started down the steps.

Jack grabbed the rope and started down. The birds' cries went on. They worried him. They sounded like warnings.

Jack reached the rocky ledge and let go of the rope.

"Let's go!" Annie called from the tree house.

Jack looked at the horizon one last time.

His heart nearly stopped. A ship was outlined against the sky! Behind it, he saw two smaller ships.

As the ships came into view, their bright sails were filled with wind and their serpent prows blazed in the new sunlight.

"Oh, no," Jack whispered. *Vikings!*

# 6

# The Vikings Are Coming!

"Annie!" Jack cried. "Vikings!"

Annie looked out the tree house window. "Vikings?"

"They're headed straight for the island!" said Jack.

He turned back to the stone steps.

"Where are you going?" cried Annie.

"To warn the monks!" Jack said.

"I'll come too!" cried Annie. She scrambled out of the tree house.

"Hurry!" said Jack.

Jack didn't even use the rope. He pulled himself up the steep steps with his hands.

As Jack and Annie climbed up the face of the cliff, clouds began to cover the sun. When they reached the top, a fog had almost hidden the serpent ships.

"Run!" cried Annie.

The fog blanketed the whole island. Jack and Annie could barely see the path to the monastery.

When they arrived at the gate, the misty white world was silent.

"Vikings!" Jack cried. "Vikings!"

"The monks are still in church!" said Annie. She yanked the bell rope.

*Dong! Dong!*

Jack and Annie watched as Brother

Patrick and the other monks ran out of the church.

"The Vikings are coming!" Jack shouted.

Brother Patrick's rosy face turned white.

"Make haste!" he said to the other monks. "Gather the books and hide."

The monks ran into the library. Brother Patrick turned to Jack and Annie.

"We have a secret hiding place, a cave on the other side of the island," he said. "You can come with us. But I am not certain you will be safe."

"Don't worry," said Jack. "We're going to try to go home."

"Do not use the steps," Brother Patrick said. "The Vikings will climb them."

"Then how do we get down?" said Jack.

"Go *that* way," said Brother Patrick, pointing. "At the cliff's edge are two large rocks. A path between those rocks will take you down to the shore. Then you can walk around to your boat."

"Thanks!" said Annie.

"Be careful!" said Brother Patrick. He hurried inside the library.

"Wait!" came a thin voice as Jack and Annie turned to run.

It was Brother Michael. He hobbled over to them, holding out his book of Irish tales.

"Take it," he said.

"Are you sure?" Jack asked. He knew it was Brother Michael's life's work.

"Please," said Brother Michael. "It is better that the world should have some of it than none at all. Just in case..."

"We'll take good care of it," said Jack. He gently placed the jeweled book in his leather bag.

"Good luck!" said Annie.

Annie and Jack waved good-bye to the old man. Then they raced to the rocks that Brother Patrick had told them about.

# 7

## Fogbound

At the rocks, the sea gulls still screeched. Jack could barely see the steep path leading down into the fog.

"Go slowly," Jack whispered to Annie as they started down.

"Whoops!" said Annie. She slipped and fell forward, bumping into Jack. "My foot got caught in my stupid dress—"

"Shh!" said Jack.

He held on to Annie. They listened as

46

pebbles and rocks rolled down the cliff.

Jack took a deep breath.

"We've got to watch out for Vikings, too," he whispered.

They started down the steep path again. They went one step at a time. The sound of the waves against the rocks grew louder.

Finally, they stepped down onto a flat strip of pebbles.

"Where are we?" whispered Annie.

"I don't know," said Jack.

"Oh, look!" said Annie. She pointed to the shoreline.

Through the fog rose the serpent prows of the Viking ships!

Jack and Annie crept closer to the ships. Their sails were down. Each ship had been tied to a tall jagged rock. They seemed deserted as they bobbed in the shallow waves.

Jack really wanted to check out the ships. But he was afraid of wasting time.

"We'd better find the tree house," he said to Annie.

They crept away from the three Viking ships.

Suddenly, they both froze.

Through the mist, they saw a group of Viking warriors. The Vikings were looking at the top of the cliff.

Their long yellow hair hung down from beneath their iron helmets. They carried round wooden shields and swords and axes.

"It looks like they're planning to climb the cliff," whispered Annie.

"We need to hide until they go," whispered Jack. "Then we can look for the tree house."

"Let's hide in a ship!" said Annie.

"Good idea," said Jack.

They crept back to where the ships were tied.

Jack was happy to see that the sides of the smallest ship were very low. They would easily be able to climb over them.

"You go first," said Annie.

Jack waded through the shallow water. It was cold!

He reached the ship and grabbed one side. He pushed himself up and onto the ship's deck.

The ship jerked forward. Jack looked at the shore. It was now thirty feet away. The ship's anchoring rope was pulled tight. The serpent prow bobbed up and down with the waves.

The fog and the movement of the ship made Jack feel as if he was in a dream. For a moment, he forgot to be scared of the Vikings.

"This is so cool," he called. "Come on, Annie!"

Annie started to wade out to the ship. Suddenly, she disappeared.

"Annie?" called Jack.

Her head popped out of the water. She splashed with her arms.

"It—it's deep!" she gasped. "My dress—too heavy!"

"Use the rope!" called Jack. "Like when we climbed the stairs!"

Annie grabbed the rope that stretched from ship to shore. It held her weight as she began inching along it.

"Hold on tight!" cried Jack.

"I—I am!" gasped Annie.

She kept going, hand over hand, along the rope, toward the ship.

When Annie got close to the ship, Jack reached out to help her. As he pulled her in, the side of the ship dipped down.

Then the rope went slack, and the Viking ship slid out to sea.

# 8

## Lost at Sea

Annie fell to the deck of the ship.

Jack pulled the rope out of the water. The end of it was still tied in a loop.

"What happened?" asked Annie.

"We're heading out to sea," said Jack. "I guess all the pulling lifted the rope off the rock."

Annie sat up and looked at the misty whiteness.

"I can't see the island," she said.

"I can't see *anything*," said Jack.

Annie looked at Jack.

"Do you think this is our darkest hour?" she asked.

"I don't know," said Jack. "Maybe the book will help."

He pulled out their research book. He found a picture of a Viking ship. He read the caption aloud:

> Viking warships were the best ships of their times. When there was no wind, the crew would take down the sails and row with oars. The smallest ships had four rowers, and the largest had as many as thirty-two. Rowers sat on boxes that stored their belongings.

"Great," said Annie, jumping up. "This *isn't* our darkest hour!"

"Why do you say that?" asked Jack.

"There's still hope," said Annie. "We can row to the other side of the island and find the tree house."

"Are you nuts?" said Jack.

"Please, Jack," said Annie. "Can we just try?"

She grabbed one of the oars. She could barely lift it.

"Forget it, Annie," said Jack. "It takes four big Viking guys to row this thing. You're too little. *I'm* too little."

"Come on, Jack. Just try," said Annie. "You get an oar, too. We'll sit on boxes across from each other."

"Oh, brother," said Jack.

Annie dragged her long oar over to a storage box.

"I'm not doing this alone," she said.

Jack groaned. Then he dragged an oar to the box across from Annie.

"Cool!" said Annie. She peered into a storage box. "Look, one for each of us!"

She lifted out two small Viking helmets.

"Maybe these were made for Viking kids who sometimes ride in this ship," said Annie.

"Maybe," said Jack.

He hadn't thought of Vikings as real people before—people with families and little kids.

Annie pulled off her scarf and put a helmet on her head.

"Now I feel like a Viking, too," she said. "I bet it will help me row."

She handed Jack a helmet. He put it on. It made him feel a little different.

"I don't know about this," he said. The helmet wasn't as heavy as the one he had worn in the time of castles. But it was still pretty heavy.

"Well, *I'm* braver with mine on," said Annie.

Jack smiled. He didn't know how Annie could be braver than she already was.

"Ready to row?" she asked.

"Yup," said Jack. He was feeling braver himself.

The wind picked up as Jack lifted his heavy oar over the side of the ship.

He lowered it into the water. But the current was so strong that the oar was ripped from his hands.

Jack fell over backward as his oar slipped into the sea.

"I lost my oar!" Annie yelled.

Jack looked up as rain started to fall. The sky was black. A gush of seawater poured over the side of the ship!

"Brrr!" said Annie as she tried to stand.

The black sky shook with thunder and flashed with lightning.

Jack crawled to the side of the ship and pulled himself up.

Another huge wave was coming right toward them!

"It's our darkest hour *now!*" cried Annie. "Get Brother Michael's book!"

Jack reached into his leather bag. He pulled out the jeweled book and held it up.

"Save us, story!" he cried.

He looked at the sea again. What he saw made him scream.

Rising from the oncoming wave was a giant sea serpent!

# 9

## Sea Monster!

The serpent's head rose higher and higher above the water.

Jack couldn't move.

"He's beautiful!" said Annie.

"Beautiful?" cried Jack.

The serpent's neck was as tall as a two-story building. Its green scales were covered with sea slime.

"Go away!" shouted Jack.

"No—stay! Help us!" shouted Annie.

The great serpent glided closer to the ship. Jack ducked.

"Come on!" said Annie. "You can do it! Get us to shore before the ship sinks!"

Jack closed his eyes. He felt the ship jerk, then move forward.

He looked up. They were gliding over the giant waves.

Jack turned. The great serpent was pressing its long neck against the back of the ship, pushing it toward the shore.

As the serpent pushed them, the wind grew calmer. The clouds lifted and the water glittered with sunlight.

The rocky shore grew closer. Jack could see the tree house on the ledge above it.

"Hurry!" Annie called to the serpent monster.

The great serpent gave the ship one last

push. The ship *swooshed* onto a sand bar near the shore.

Jack put the jeweled book carefully back into his bag. Then he and Annie climbed out of the ship onto the wet sand. They looked back at the sea.

The great serpent was rearing its long neck into the air. Its scales glittered pink and green in the sunlight.

"Bye!" shouted Annie. "Thanks a lot!"

The monster seemed to nod at her. Then he dove into the sea and was gone.

Jack and Annie headed toward the rocks. All of a sudden, Annie gasped.

"Uh-oh," she said, pointing to the top of the cliff.

Two Vikings were staring down at them!

"To the tree house!" cried Jack.

The Vikings shouted and started down the steep stairs.

Jack and Annie began scrambling up the rocks.

They reached the tree house and climbed inside.

Jack grabbed the Pennsylvania book.

Annie stuck her head out the window.

"Go home! Stop causing trouble!" she yelled to the Vikings, who were almost to the ledge.

Jack pointed at the picture of the Frog Creek woods.

"IWISHWECOULDGOTHERE!" Jack shouted.

Just as the Vikings reached the ledge, the wind began to blow.

The tree house started to spin.

It spun faster and faster.

Then everything was still.

Absolutely still.

# 10

## Sunrise

"Boy, I'm glad to be back in my jeans," said Annie.

Jack opened his eyes. He still felt damp. But he was glad to be wearing his jeans again, too.

"Welcome home," said Morgan. She was standing in the shadows. "Are you all right?"

"Of course!" piped Annie.

"And we brought back the lost book," said Jack.

He reached in his backpack and took out the jeweled book of Brother Michael. He handed it to Morgan.

The enchantress sighed. She ran her hand over the sparkling cover.

"A great work of art," she said.

Morgan then put the book next to the scroll from Roman times and the bamboo book from ancient China.

"I'm afraid the story you wanted is not all there," said Jack. "Brother Michael didn't get the chance to finish it."

Morgan nodded.

"I know," she said. "Sadly, we have only bits and pieces of many wonderful old stories."

"What's the story about?" asked Annie.

"It's an ancient Irish tale about a great

serpent named Sarph," said Morgan.

"He saved us by pushing our ship over the stormy waves!" Annie said.

"Sarph was a huge, ugly monster," said Jack.

Morgan smiled.

"Sometimes monsters can be heroes," she said.

"What about Vikings?" asked Jack.

"Oh, most definitely, Vikings could be heroes, too," she said. "In fact, once the Vikings settled down, they became more than just a warrior people. They actually added a lot to civilization."

"We found *civilization* on our trip," said Annie.

"Yeah," said Jack, "in the library of the monastery."

Morgan smiled again.

"Their library was a light in the Dark Ages, wasn't it?" she said.

Jack nodded. He thought of Brother Michael and the other monks making their beautiful books by candlelight.

"Thank you also for your great courage," Morgan said. "You are both heroes, too."

Jack smiled shyly.

"Go home now and rest," said Morgan.

"Bye," Jack and Annie said together.

They started down the tree house ladder. The sky was turning pink and gold.

When they reached the ground, Morgan called out to them, "Come back in two weeks. I need you to find one more lost book."

"Where is it?" said Jack.

"Ancient Greece," said Morgan. "A place

with the highest civilization—*and* the first Olympic games."

"Oh, wow!" said Annie.

Jack was thrilled. He had always wanted to go to ancient Greece.

Jack and Annie took off through the woods.

The sun was rising when they got to their front porch.

Annie opened the front door. She stuck her head inside and listened.

"Everything's quiet," she whispered. "I think Mom and Dad are still sleeping."

She moved quietly inside.

Jack turned back to watch the red sun rise through a clear blue sky.

He thought about how it was the same sun that had risen in Ireland—over a thousand years ago.

"Shine, O light of the sun," Jack whispered, "on this day filled with wonder."

Then he slipped inside his quiet house.

# MORE FACTS FOR YOU AND JACK

1) In the fifth century, St. Patrick converted Ireland to Christianity. Scholars and craftsmen from all over Europe studied with the Irish monks in their monasteries.

2) Monks in the monasteries made beautiful manuscripts to reflect the glory of God. Most of their manuscripts were religious in nature.

3) The first recorded people of Ireland were the Celts. Before the Irish became Christians, they practiced the Celtic religion and developed a Celtic mythology.

4) The great sea serpent Sarph was a Celtic creature who was identified with the Milky Way. Just as Jack and Annie were not able to rescue the complete story of Sarph, today we

have only fragments of many old Celtic stories.

5) The word *Vikings* means "fighting men." Vikings included Danes, Norwegians, and Swedes.

6) In the ninth century, Viking raiders attacked the coastal villages of England, Scotland, and Ireland, stealing treasure and carrying people off to be slaves.

7) The Vikings were the greatest shipbuilders of their time. The shallowness of their warships allowed them to land on most beaches.

8) The Vikings were "settling men" as well as "fighting men." Eventually they settled down in Europe and became traders, exchanging goods rather than stealing them. They were also expert craftsmen.

Don't miss the next Magic Tree House book,
when Jack and Annie are whisked back
to ancient Greece and the very first
Olympic Games in

# MAGIC TREE HOUSE #16

## HOUR OF
## THE OLYMPICS

(October 1998)

# Where have you traveled in the

# MAGIC TREE HOUSE ?

## The Mystery of the Tree House
## (Books #1–4)

❑ **Magic Tree House #1, Dinosaurs Before Dark,**
in which Jack and Annie discover the tree house and
travel back to the time of dinosaurs.

❑ **Magic Tree House #2, The Knight at Dawn,**
in which Jack and Annie go to the time of knights
and explore a medieval castle with a hidden passage.

❑ **Magic Tree House #3, Mummies in the Morning,**
in which Jack and Annie go to ancient Egypt and get
lost in a pyramid when they help a ghost queen.

❑ **Magic Tree House #4, Pirates Past Noon,**
in which Jack and Annie travel back in time and meet
some unfriendly pirates searching for buried treasure.

## The Mystery of the Magic Spell
## (Books #5–8)

❑ **Magic Tree House #5, NIGHT OF THE NINJAS,** in which Jack and Annie go to old Japan and learn the secrets of the ninjas.

❑ **Magic Tree House #6, AFTERNOON ON THE AMAZON,** in which Jack and Annie explore the wild rain forest of the Amazon and are greeted by giant ants, hungry crocodiles, and flesh-eating piranhas.

❑ **Magic Tree House #7, SUNSET OF THE SABERTOOTH,** in which Jack and Annie go back to the Ice Age—the world of woolly mammoths, sabertooth tigers, and a mysterious sorcerer.

❑ **Magic Tree House #8, MIDNIGHT ON THE MOON,** in which Jack and Annie go forward in time and explore the moon in a moon buggy.

# The Mystery of the Ancient Riddles
## (Books #9–12)

❑ **Magic Tree House #9, DOLPHINS AT DAYBREAK,** in which Jack and Annie arrive on a coral reef, where they find a mini-submarine that takes them underwater into the world of sharks and dolphins.

❑ **Magic Tree House #10, GHOST TOWN AT SUNDOWN,** in which Jack and Annie travel to the Wild West, where they battle horse thieves, meet a kindly cowboy, and get some help from a mysterious ghost.

❑ **Magic Tree House #11, LIONS AT LUNCHTIME,** in which Jack and Annie go to the plains of Africa, where they help wild animals cross a rushing river and have a picnic with a Masai warrior.

❑ **Magic Tree House #12, POLAR BEARS PAST BEDTIME,** in which Jack and Annie go to the Arctic, where they get help from a seal hunter, play with polar bear cubs, and get trapped on thin ice.

## The Mystery of the Lost Stories
## (Books #13–16)

☐ **Magic Tree House #13, VACATION ON THE VOLCANO,** in which Jack and Annie land in Pompeii during Roman times, on the very day Mount Vesuvius erupts!

☐ **Magic Tree House #14, DAY OF THE DRAGON KING,** in which Jack and Annie travel back to ancient China, where they must face an emperor who burns books.

☐ **Magic Tree House #15, VIKING SHIPS AT SUNRISE,** in which Jack and Annie visit a monastery in medieval Ireland on the day the Vikings attack!

☐ **Magic Tree House #16, HOUR OF THE OLYMPICS,** in which Jack and Annie are whisked back to ancient Greece and the first Olympic games.

# Read all the Magic Tree House books!

**Available wherever books are sold...OR**
**You can send in this coupon (with check or money order)**
**and have the books mailed directly to you!**

☐ #1: Dinosaurs Before Dark (0-679-82411-1)    $3.99

☐ #2: The Knight at Dawn (0-679-82412-X)    $3.99

☐ #3: Mummies in the Morning (0-679-82424-3)    $3.99

☐ #4: Pirates Past Noon (0-679-82425-1)    $3.99

☐ #5: Night of the Ninjas (0-679-86371-0)    $3.99

☐ #6: Afternoon on the Amazon (0-679-86372-9)    $3.99

☐ #7: Sunset of the Sabertooth (0-679-86373-7)    $3.99

☐ #8: Midnight on the Moon (0-679-86374-5)    $3.99

☐ #9: Dolphins at Daybreak (0-679-88338-X)    $3.99

☐ #10: Ghost Town at Sundown (0-679-88339-8)    $3.99

☐ #11: Lions at Lunchtime (0-679-88340-1)    $3.99

☐ #12: Polar Bears Past Bedtime (0-679-88341-X)    $3.99

☐ #13: Vacation Under the Volcano (0-679-89050-5)    $3.99

☐ #14: Day of the Dragon King (0-679-89051-3)    $3.99

Subtotal ........................................$ _____
Shipping and handling............................$   3.00
Sales tax (where applicable)......................
Total amount enclosed............................$ _____

Name _____

Address _____

City _____ State _____ Zip _____

Prices and numbers subject to change without notice. Valid in U.S. only.
All orders subject to availability. Please allow 4 to 6 weeks for delivery.

Make your check or money order (no cash or C.O.D.s)
payable to Random House, Inc., and mail to:
Magic Tree House Mail Sales, 400 Hahn Road, Westminster, MD 21157.

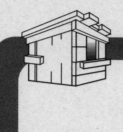

**Visit the**

## MAGIC TREE HOUSE

**website**

**at**

www.randomhouse.com/magictreehouse/

# DATE DUE

|  |  |  |  |
|---|---|---|---|
|  |  |  |  |
|  |  |  |  |
|  |  |  |  |
|  |  |  |  |
|  |  |  |  |
|  |  |  |  |
|  |  |  |  |
|  |  |  |  |
|  |  |  |  |
|  |  |  |  |
|  |  |  |  |
|  |  |  |  |
|  |  |  |  |
|  |  |  |  |
|  |  |  |  |
|  |  |  |  |
|  |  |  |  |